THE STORY OF
SPIDER-MAN

Adapted by Thomas Macri
Illustrated by The Storybook Art Group
Based on the Marvel comic book series The Amazing Spider-Man

ABDO
Spotlight

MARVEL
New York

WWW.ABDOPUBLISHING.COM

Reinforced library bound edition published in 2015 by Spotlight, a division of ABDO
PO Box 398166, Minneapolis, Minnesota 55439. Spotlight produces high-quality
reinforced library bound editions for schools and libraries. Published by
Marvel Press, an imprint of Disney Book Group.

Printed in the United States of America, North Mankato, Minnesota.
052014
072014

marvelkids.com
TM & © 2012 Marvel & Subs.

THIS BOOK CONTAINS
RECYCLED MATERIALS

LIBRARY OF CONGRESS CATALOGING-IN-PUBLICATION DATA

This title was previously cataloged with the following information:

Macri, Thomas.
The story of Spider-Man / adapted by Thomas Macri ; illustrated by The Storybook Art
Group.
   p. cm. -- (World of reading. Level 2)
Summary: Tells the story of Peter Parker, a normal teenage boy who, when bitten by
a radioactive spider and given spider-like super powers, decides to fight crime as the
superhero Spider-Man.
1. Spider-Man (Fictitious character)--Juvenile fiction. 2. Superheroes--Juvenile fiction. I.
Storybook Art Group, ill. II. Title. III. Series.
PZ7.M24731St 2012
[E]--dc23

                          2012285590

978-1-61479-260-4 (Reinforced Library Bound Edition)

Spotlight
A Division of ABDO
www.abdopublishing.com

Peter Parker didn't have
many friends.

Other kids thought Peter was
different. They made fun of him.
They liked sports and music.
Peter liked books.

Peter loved all his classes at school. But he loved science the most.

Peter only loved one thing more than science. He loved his family. He lived with his Aunt May and his Uncle Ben. At home, Peter couldn't have been happier.

Aunt May and Uncle Ben loved Peter.
They bought him a new microscope.
Uncle Ben told him that science was
power. "And," he said, "with great
power comes great responsibility."

One day, Peter heard that a lab was going to do something special. They were going to show how rays worked. Peter visited the lab to see it.

The rays lit up. But a spider dropped down between them.

The spider was zapped with power.

Peter didn't notice something.
The spider was falling down. And
it was falling on him!

The spider was glowing with power.
It bit Peter's hand.

Peter held his head. He felt sick.

Peter left the lab. He felt so sick that he almost didn't see a car coming.

He jumped out of the way.

He jumped higher than he thought
he could. He landed on a wall.
And he stuck to it!

He climbed up the wall. He was just like the spider that bit him!

He jumped from roof to roof. His powers were like a spider's.
He must have gotten them from the spider's bite!

Peter was amazed by his powers.

Peter saw a poster of a wrestler.
He would test his powers on him.

Peter put on a mask. He challenged the wrestler.

He threw the wrestler.

He beat the wrestler!

Peter was happy. But he couldn't be a spider-man without something else. He went home and made some gluey stuff.

Then he made something to shoot the stuff. He called them web-shooters.

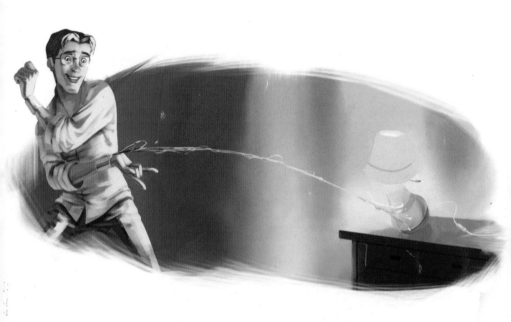

Peter made a costume. He called himself Spider-Man!

People loved Spider-Man! They loved his powers. Soon he was famous.

But one night he saw a robbery
taking place. A cop called out to
stop the crook. But Peter didn't
stop him. Peter was tired of being
told what to do. So he let the
crook go.

Peter went home. There were cops
outside. He knew something
was wrong. The cops told Peter
there had been a crime at his house.
Uncle Ben was the victim.

Peter put on his Spider-Man costume.

He rushed to find the criminal.

When he found him, Peter discovered
something terrible. The crook was
the same man he had let run away.

Peter was so sad he cried. But he remembered that Uncle Ben had told him with great power comes great responsibility.

He knew this meant he had to fight crime. He would do it as Spider-Man. He swung over the city.
A hero had been born.

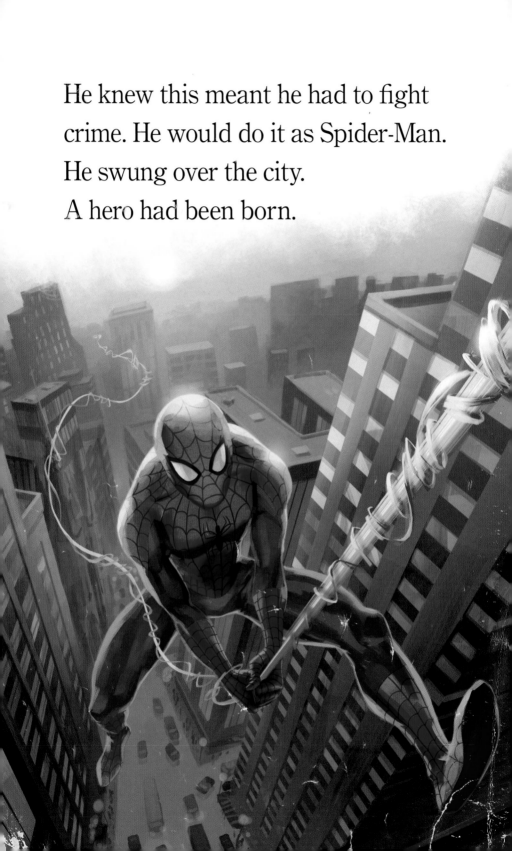